A. A. MILNE

Tiggers
Don't
Climb Trees

illustrated by
E. H. SHEPARD

DUTTON CHILDREN'S BOOKS

the third stone he began to wonder how Kanga
and Roo and Tigger were getting on, because
they all lived together in a different part of

Tiggers Don't Climb Trees

One day when Pooh was thinking, he thought he
would go and see Eeyore, because he hadn't
seen him since yesterday. And as he walked
through the heather, singing to himself, he
suddenly remembered that he hadn't seen Owl
since the day before yesterday, so he thought
that he would just look in at the Hundred Acre
Wood on the way and see if Owl was at home.

Well, he went on singing, until he came to
the part of the stream where the stepping-
stones were, and when he was in the middle of

the Forest. And he thought, 'I haven't seen
Roo for a long time, and if I don't see him
to-day it will be a still longer time.' So
he sat down on the stone in the middle of the
stream, and sang another verse of his song,
while he wondered what to do.

The other verse of the song was like
this:

> I could spend a happy morning
>   Seeing Roo,
> I could spend a happy morning
>   Being Pooh.
> For it doesn't seem to matter,
> If I don't get any fatter
> (And I *don't* get any fatter),
>   What I do.

The sun was so delightfully warm, and the
stone, which had been sitting in it for a long
time, was so warm, too, that Pooh had almost
decided to go on being Pooh in the middle of

the stream for the rest of the morning, when he remembered Rabbit.

'Rabbit,' said Pooh to himself. 'I *like* talking to Rabbit. He talks about sensible things. He doesn't use long, difficult words, like Owl. He uses short, easy words, like "What about lunch?" and "Help yourself, Pooh," I suppose, *really*, I ought to go and see Rabbit.'

Which made him think of another verse:

> Oh, I like his way of talking,
>   Yes, I do.
> It's the nicest way of talking
>   Just for two.
> And a Help-yourself with Rabbit
> Though it may become a habit,
> Is a *pleasant* sort of habit
>   For a Pooh.

So when he had sung this, he got up off his stone, walked back across the stream, and set off for Rabbit's house.

But he hadn't got far before he began to say to himself: 'Yes, but suppose Rabbit is out?'

'Or suppose I get stuck in his front door again, coming out, as I did once when his front door wasn't big enough?'

'Because I *know* I'm not getting fatter, but his front door may be getting thinner.'

'So wouldn't it be better if—'

And all the time he was saying things like this he was going more and more westerly, without thinking . . . until suddenly he found himself at his own front door again.

And it was eleven o'clock.

Which was Time-for-a-little-something. . . .

Half an hour later he was doing what he had always really meant to do, he was stumping off to Piglet's house. And as he walked, he

wiped his mouth with the back of his paw, and
sang rather a fluffy song through the fur. It
went like this:

   I could spend a happy morning
     Seeing Piglet.
   And I couldn't spend a happy morning
     Not seeing Piglet.
   And it doesn't seem to matter
   If I don't see Owl and Eeyore (or any of the others),
   And I'm not going to see Owl or Eeyore (or any of
     the others)
   Or Christopher Robin.

   Written down like this, it doesn't seem
a very good song, but coming through pale fawn
fluff at about half-past eleven on a very
sunny morning, it seemed to Pooh to be one of
the best songs he had ever sung. So he went on
singing it.
   Piglet was busy digging a small hole in
the ground outside his house.

'Hallo, Piglet,' said Pooh.

'Hallo, Pooh,' said Piglet, giving a jump of surprise. 'I knew it was you.'

'So did I,' said Pooh. 'What are you doing?'

'I'm planting a haycorn, Pooh, so that it can grow up into an oak-tree, and have lots of haycorns just outside the front door instead of having to walk miles and miles, do you see, Pooh?

'Supposing it doesn't?' said Pooh.

'It will, because Christopher Robin says it will, so that's why I'm planting it.'

'Well,' said Pooh, 'if I plant a honeycomb outside my house, then it will grow up into a beehive.'

Piglet wasn't quite sure about this.

'Or a *piece* of a honeycomb,' said Pooh, 'so as not to waste too much. Only then I might only get a piece of a beehive, and it might be the wrong piece, where the bees were buzzing and not hunnying. Bother.'

Piglet agreed that that would be rather bothering.

'Besides, Pooh, it's a very difficult thing, planting unless you know how to do it,' he said; and he put the acorn in the hole he had made, and covered it up with earth, and jumped on it.

'I do know,' said Pooh, 'because Christopher Robin gave me a mastershalum seed, and I planted it, and I'm going to have mastershalums all over the front door.'

'I thought they were called nasturtiums,' said Piglet timidly, as he went on jumping.

'No,' said Pooh. 'Not these. These are called mastershalums.'

When Piglet had finished jumping, he wiped his paws on his front, and said, 'What shall we do now?' and Pooh said, 'Let's go and see Kanga and Roo and Tigger,' and Piglet said 'Y-yes. L-let's'—because he was still a little anxious about Tigger, who was a very Bouncy Animal, with a way of saying How-do-you-do, which always left your ears full of sand, even after Kanga had said, 'Gently, Tigger dear,' and had helped you up again. So they set off for Kanga's house.

Now it happened that Kanga had felt rather motherly that morning, and Wanting to Count Things—like Roo's vests, and how many pieces of soap there were left, and the two clean

spots in Tigger's feeder; so she had sent them
out with a packet of watercress sandwiches for
Roo and a packet of extract-of-malt sandwiches
for Tigger, to have a nice long morning in
the Forest not getting into mischief. And off
they had gone.

And as they went, Tigger told Roo (who
wanted to know) all about the things that
Tiggers could do.

'Can they fly?' asked Roo.

'Yes,' said Tigger, 'they're very good
flyers, Tiggers are. Strornry good flyers.'

'Oo!' said Roo. 'Can they fly as well as Owl?'

'Yes,' said Tigger. 'Only they don't want to.'

'Why don't they want to?'

'Well, they just don't like it, somehow.'

Roo couldn't understand this, because he
thought it would be lovely to be able to fly,
but Tigger said it was difficult to explain to
anybody who wasn't a Tigger himself.

'Well,' said Roo, 'can they jump as far
as Kangas?'

'Yes,' said Tigger. 'When they want to.'

'I *love* jumping,' said Roo. 'Let see who can jump farthest, you or me.'

'*I* can,' said Tigger. 'But we mustn't stop now, or we shall be late.'

'Late for what?'

'For whatever we want to be in time for,' said Tigger, hurrying on.

In a little while they came to the Six Pine Trees.

'I can swim,' said Roo. 'I fell into the river, and I swimmed. Can Tiggers swim?'

'Of course they can. Tiggers can do everything.'

'Can they climb trees better than Pooh?' asked Roo, stopping under the tallest Pine Tree, and looking up at it.

'Climbing trees is what they do best,' said Tigger. 'Much better than Poohs.'

'Could they climb this one?'

'They're always climbing trees like that,' said Tigger. 'Up and down all day.'

'Oo, Tigger, are they *really*?'

'I'll show you,' said Tigger bravely, 'and
you can sit on my back and watch me.' For of
all the things which he had said Tiggers could
do, the only one he felt really certain about
suddenly was climbing trees.

'Oo, Tigger—oo, Tigger—oo, Tigger!'
squeaked Roo excitedly.

So he sat on Tigger's back and up they went.

And for the first ten feet Tigger said
happily to himself, 'Up we go!'

And for the next ten feet he said: 'I always
said Tiggers could climb trees.'

And for the next ten feet he said: 'Not that
it's easy, mind you.'

And for the next ten feet he said: 'Of course,
there's the coming-down too. Backwards.'

And then he said: 'Which will be
difficult . . .'

'Unless one fell . . .'

'When it would be . . .'

'EASY.'

And at the word 'easy', the branch he was standing on broke suddenly and he just managed to clutch at the one above him as he felt himself going . . . and then slowly he got his chin over it . . . and then one back paw . . . and then the other . . . until at last he was sitting on it, breathing very quickly, and wishing that he had gone in for swimming instead.

Roo climbed off, and sat down next to him.

'Oo, Tigger,' he said excitedly, 'are we at the top?'

'No,' said Tigger.

'Are we going to the top?'

'*No*,' said Tigger.

'Oh!' said Roo rather sadly. And then he went on hopefully: 'That was a lovely bit just now, when you pretended we were going to fall-bump-to-the-bottom, and we didn't. Will you do that bit again?'

'NO,' said Tigger.

Roo was silent for a little while, and then he said, 'Shall we eat our sandwiches, Tigger?' And

Tigger said, 'Yes, where are they?' And Roo said, 'At the bottom of the tree.'

And Tigger said, 'I don't think we'd better eat them just yet.'

So they didn't.

By-and-by Pooh and Piglet came along. Pooh was telling Piglet in a singing voice that it didn't seem to matter, if he didn't get any fatter, and he didn't *think* he was getting any fatter, what he did; and Piglet was wondering how long it would be before his haycorn came up.

'Look, Pooh!' said Piglet suddenly. 'There's something in one of the Pine Trees.'

'So there is!' said Pooh, looking up wonderingly. 'There's an Animal.'

Piglet took Pooh's arm, in case Pooh was frightened. 'Is it One of the Fiercer Animals?' he said, looking the other way.

Pooh nodded. 'It's a Jagular,' he said.

'What do Jagulars do?' asked Piglet, hoping that they wouldn't.

'They hide in the branches of trees and drop on you as you go underneath,' said Pooh. 'Christopher Robin told me.'

'Perhaps we better hadn't go underneath, Pooh. In case he dropped and hurt himself.'

'They don't hurt themselves,' said Pooh. 'They're such very good droppers.'

Piglet still felt that to be underneath a Very Good Dropper would be a Mistake, and he

was just going to hurry back for something
which he had forgotten when the Jagular
called out to them.

'Help! Help!' it called.

'That's what Jagulars always do,' said Pooh,
much interested. 'They call "Help! Help!" and
then when you look up, they drop on you.'

'I'm looking *down*,' cried Piglet loudly, so as
the Jagular shouldn't do the wrong thing by
accident.

Something very excited next to the Jagular
heard him, and squeaked: 'Pooh and Piglet!
Pooh and Piglet!'

All of a sudden Piglet felt that it was a
much nicer day than he had thought it was. All
warm and sunny—

'Pooh!' he cried. 'I believe it's Tigger and Roo!'

'So it is,' said Pooh. 'I thought it was a
Jagular and another Jagular.'

'Hallo, Roo!' called Piglet. 'What are you
doing?'

'We can't get down, we can't get down!' cried

Roo. 'Isn't it fun? Pooh, isn't it fun, Tigger and I are living in a tree, like Owl, and we're going to stay here for ever and ever. I can see Piglet's house. Piglet, I can see your house from here. Aren't we high? Is Owl's house as high up as this?'

'How did you get there, Roo?' asked Piglet.

'On Tigger's back! And Tiggers can't climb downwards, because their tails get in the way, only upwards, and Tigger forgot about that when

we started, and he's only just remembered. So
we've got to stay here for ever and ever—
unless we go higher. What did you say, Tigger?
Oh, Tigger says if we go higher we shan't be
able to see Piglet's house so well, so we're
going to stop here.'

'Piglet,' said Pooh solemnly, when he had
heard all this, 'what shall we do?' And he began
to eat Tigger's sandwiches.

'Are they stuck?' asked Piglet anxiously.

Pooh nodded.

'Couldn't you climb up to them?'

'I might, Piglet, and I might bring Roo down

on my back, but I couldn't bring Tigger down. So we must think of something else.' And in a thoughtful way he began to eat Roo's sandwiches, too.

Whether he would have thought of anything before he had finished the last sandwich, I don't know, but he had just got to the last but one when there was a crackling in the bracken, and Christopher Robin and Eeyore came strolling along together.

'I shouldn't be surprised if it hailed a good deal to-morrow,' Eeyore was saying. 'Blizzards and what-not. Being fine to-day doesn't Mean Anything. It has no sig—what's that word? Well, it has none of that. It's just a small piece of weather.'

'There's Pooh!' said Christopher Robin, who didn't much mind *what* it did to-morrow, as long as he was out in it. 'Hallo, Pooh!'

'It's Christopher Robin!'

said Piglet. '*He'll* know what to do.'

They hurried up to him.

'Oh, Christopher Robin,' began Pooh.

'And Eeyore,' said Eeyore.

'Tigger and Roo are right up the Six Pine Trees, and they can't get down, and—'

'And I was just saying,' put in Piglet, 'that if only Christopher Robin—'

'*And* Eeyore—'

'If only you were here, then we could think of something to do.'

Christopher Robin looked up at Tigger and Roo, and tried to think of something.

'*I* thought,' said Piglet earnestly, 'that if Eeyore stood at the bottom of the tree, and if Pooh stood on Eeyore's back, and if I stood on Pooh's shoulders—'

'And if Eeyore's back snapped suddenly, then we could all laugh. Ha ha! Amusing in a quiet way,' said Eeyore, 'but not really helpful.'

'Well,' said Piglet meekly, '*I* thought—'

'Would it break your back, Eeyore?' asked

Pooh, very much surprised.

'That's what would be so interesting, Pooh. Not being quite sure till afterwards.'

Pooh said 'Oh!' and they all began to think again.

'I've got an idea!' cried Christopher Robin suddenly.

'Listen to this, Piglet,' said Eeyore, 'and then you'll know what we're trying to do.'

'I'll take off my tunic and we'll each hold a corner, and then Roo and Tigger can jump into it, and it will be all soft and bouncy for them, and they won't hurt themselves.'

'*Getting Tigger down*,' said Eeyore, 'and *Not hurting anybody*. Keep those two ideas in your head, Piglet, and you'll be all right.'

But Piglet wasn't listening, he was so agog at the thought of seeing Christopher Robin's blue braces again. He had only seen them once before, when he was much younger, and, being a little over-excited by them, had had to go to bed half an hour earlier than usual; and he had always wondered since if they were *really* as blue and as bracing as he had thought them. So when Christopher Robin took his tunic off, and they were, he felt quite friendly to Eeyore again, and held the corner of the tunic next to him and smiled happily at him. And Eeyore whispered back: 'I'm not saying there won't be an Accident *now*, mind you. They're funny things, Accidents. You never have them till you're having them.'

When Roo understood what he had to do, he was wildly excited and cried out: 'Tigger, Tigger, we're going to jump! Look at me jumping, Tigger! Like flying, my jumping will be. Can Tiggers do it?' And he squeaked out: 'I'm com-ing, Christopher Robin!' and he jumped—straight into the middle of the tunic. And he was going so fast that he bounced up again almost as high as where he was before—and he went on bouncing and saying, 'Oo!' for quite a long time — and then at last he stopped and said, 'Oo, lovely!' And they put him on the ground.

'Come on, Tigger,' he called out. 'It's easy.'

But Tigger was holding on to the branch and saying to himself: 'It's all very well for Jumping Animals like Kangas, but it's quite different for Swimming Animals like Tiggers.' And he thought of himself floating on his back down a river, or striking out from one island to another, and he felt that that was really the life for a Tigger.

'Come along,' called Christopher Robin. 'You'll be all right.'

'Just wait a moment,' said Tigger nervously. 'Small piece of bark in my eye.' And he moved slowly along his branch.

'Come on, it's easy!' squeaked Roo. And suddenly Tigger found how easy it was.

'Ow!' he shouted as the tree flew past him.

'Look out!' cried Christopher Robin to the others.

There was a crash, and a tearing noise, and a confused heap of everybody on the ground.

Christopher Robin and Pooh and Piglet picked themselves up first, and then they picked Tigger up, and underneath everybody else was Eeyore.

'Oh, Eeyore!' cried Christopher Robin. 'Are you hurt?' And he felt him rather anxiously, and dusted him and helped him to stand up again.

Eeyore said nothing for a long time. And then he said: 'Is Tigger there?'

Tigger was there, feeling Bouncy again already.

'Yes,' said Christopher Robin. 'Tigger's here.'

'Well, just thank him for me,' said Eeyore.